THERE'S A GONG IN MY FISHBOWL

By Anthony J. Cirone and Marie Colligan • Illustrations by Daniel Evans
Music composed and performed by Elizabeth Ann Bongiorno • Vocals, Timpani,
and Percussion by Anthony M. Bongionro

AuthorHouse™
1663 Liberty Drive
Bloomington, IN 47403
www.authorhouse.com
Phone: 833-262-8899

This book is printed on acid-free paper.

ISBN: 978-1-6655-3719-3 (sc)
ISBN: 978-1-6655-3720-9 (e)

Print information available on the last page.

Published by AuthorHouse 11/17/2021

authorHOUSE

INTRODUCTION

The idea of creating <u>There's A Gong In My Fishbowl</u> as a children's book came from an actual event during the 1970s when the San Francisco Symphony was performing a concert of Avant-Garde music. One of the works involved a percussionist striking a Gong and placing it in and out of a tub of water to produce and unusual modulation of the Gong sound. The tub of water had to be brought on and off stage by the Stage Crew for each rehearsal and concert. They were not too happy about this and decided to put a goldfish into the tub right before the first performance.

As the concert was soon to start, my colleague from the Percussion Section went to the front of the stage where the tub of water was placed a few minutes before the downbeat was to occur. Seeing the goldfish in the tub, he looked back at the percussion section, smiling as he pointed to the tub of water. We had no idea what he was smiling about.

The concert began, and at the proper moment he struck the Gong and slowly placed it into the water. As he told us after the performance, the goldfish began swimming rapidly in the water and jumping up and down when the vibrations occurred. Meanwhile the Stage Crew were offstage watching this event and getting a good laugh of the expressions on the percussionist's face. By the end of the performance the goldfish died.

My cousin Marie Colligan read about this event in my book titled: <u>The Great American Symphony Orchestra</u>. Being a writer herself, she told me this story would make a great children's book. That began the process of <u>There's a Gong in my Fishbowl.</u> But, please don't be alarmed, the goldfish does not die in OUR story!

Anthony J. Cirone

Since this entire book is set to music, please place the camera of your Cell Phone on the QR Square below to download the file to hear the Mini Operetta as you follow along in the book.

2.

They exchange some exuberant

happy "high-fives"

and await the conductor

who soon will arrive.

Moderato ♩. = 80

They ex - change some ex - u - ber - ant hap - py "high fives" and a -

wait the con - duc - tor who soon will ar - rive.

3.

A trio of monkeys

then break into song,

and dance on the Xylophone

and swing from the Gong.

Sliding Trombones make loud ear-spliting tones,

while Drums and the Strings

practice hard to learn things.

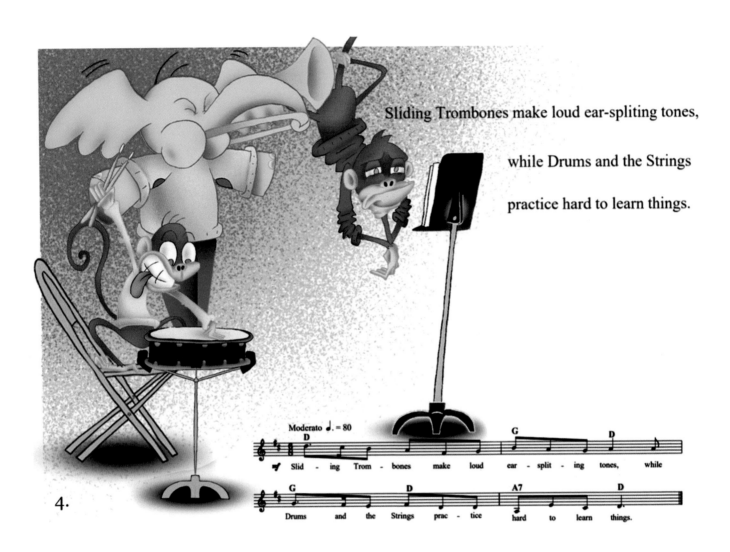

4.

Each octopus plays two violins at a time,

the sound is confusing but not a big crime.

When their arms get all tangled

and the bow hairs are mangled,

it's a wonder that none of the

players get strangled!

5.

The Music Director, a shiny black crow, now enters the stage and is called the "Maestro."
We know he's the boss, and he often gets cross, when musical notes sometimes seem to get

lost.

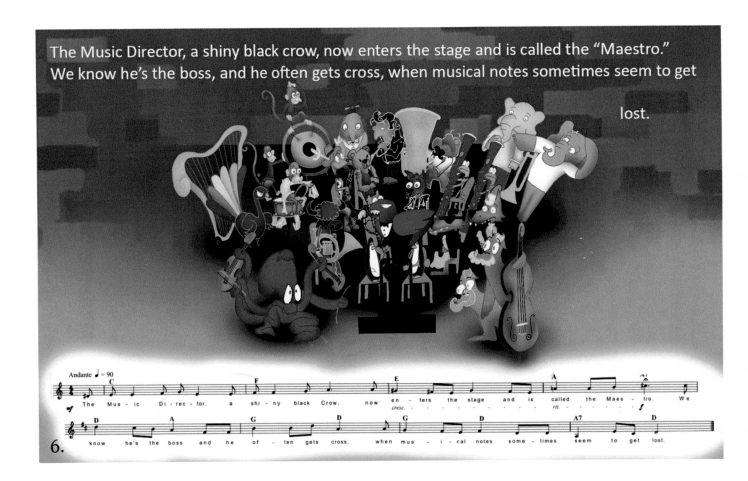

Miss Peacock embraces
the strings of the Harp,
and breaks one
because her long claws are so sharp.

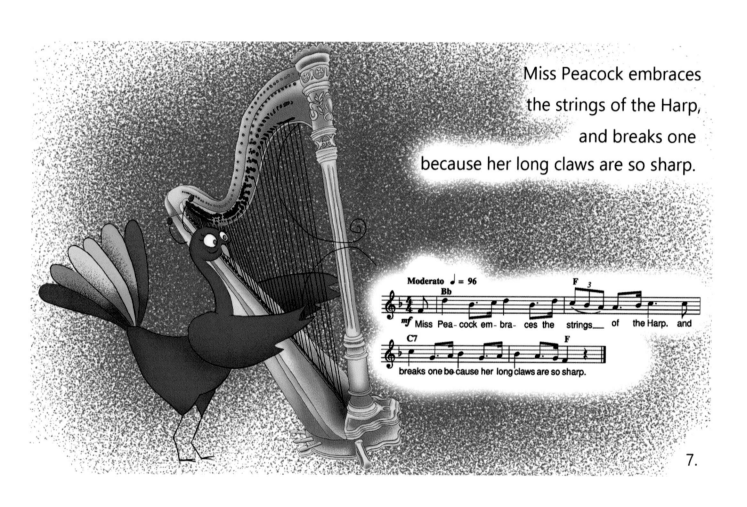

The gray and the red fox play Sax to the max,
and bounce 'cross the stage like two crazed jumping jacks.

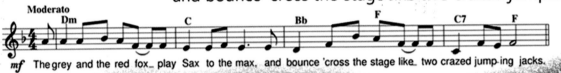

Moderato

mf The grey and the red fox_ play Sax to the max, and bounce 'cross the stage like_ two crazed jump-ing jacks.

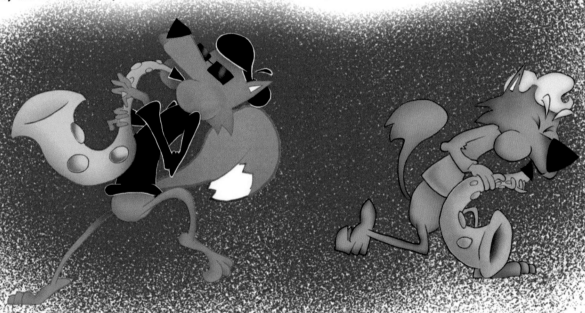

8.

When elephants and hippos

blow into their Horns,

out comes an explosion of

hot buttered popcorn.

9.

"Clarinet! Oboe! And you, too, Miss Flute!

I'd sure like to hear all your very best toot.

Miss Piccolo, your B-flat is simply too sharp.

Please tune up before the next time that you start."

Andante ♩ = 50

Clar-i-net! O-boe And you too Miss Flute! I'd sure like to hear all your ve-ry best toot." Miss

Picc-o-lo, your B-flat is sim-ply too sharp. Please tune up be-fore the next time that you start."

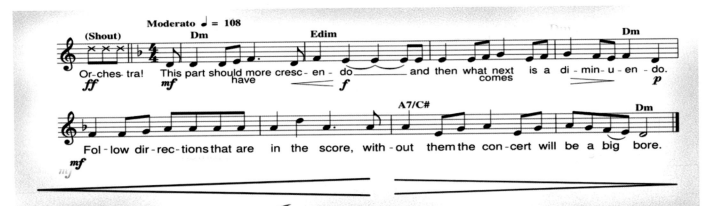

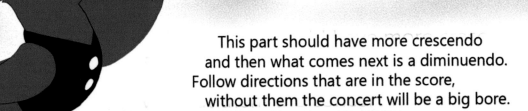

"Orchestra!"

This part should have more crescendo
and then what comes next is a diminuendo.
Follow directions that are in the score,
without them the concert will be a big bore.

12.

"Snare Drum! Don't rush 'cause you're not with the beat." "Trumpet! I've asked you to stay in your seats."

"Strings!"
   "The soft music should flow like a waltz,
   not a cool hip-hop type Be-bop of course."

The working rehearsal has finally ended, but certainly not as the Maestro intended.

The animals felt they should all be commended, to them the rehearsal was just ding-dong splendid.

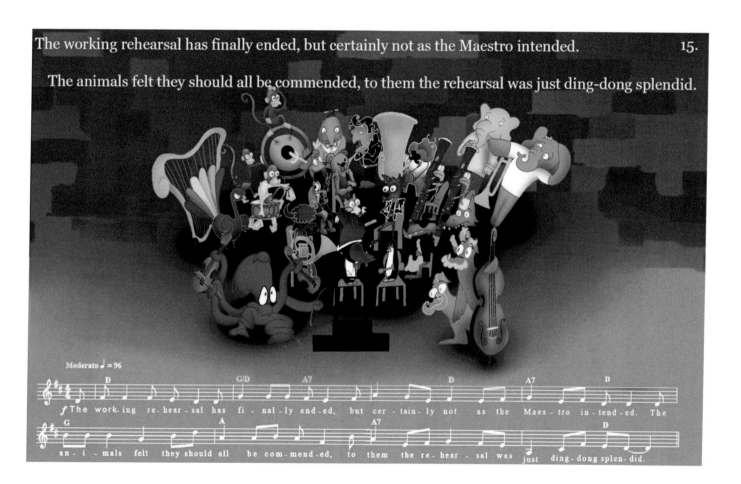

As the moment arrived for the concert to start, the musicians warm up and do look very smart.
Dressed up in tuxedos or long evening gowns, they're excited to start making musical sounds.

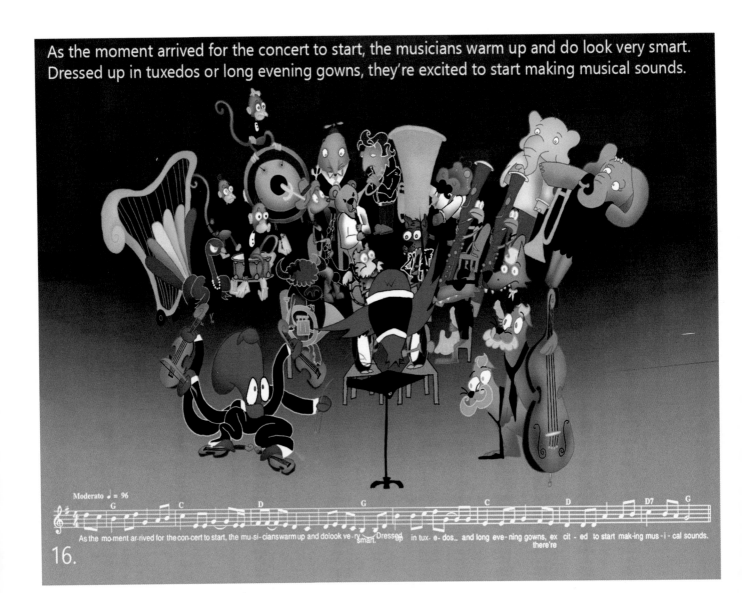

16.

But unknown to all, sneaking into the Hall, the
monkeys bring with them a great big glass bowl
that holds their pet fish who's so shiny and gold.

17.

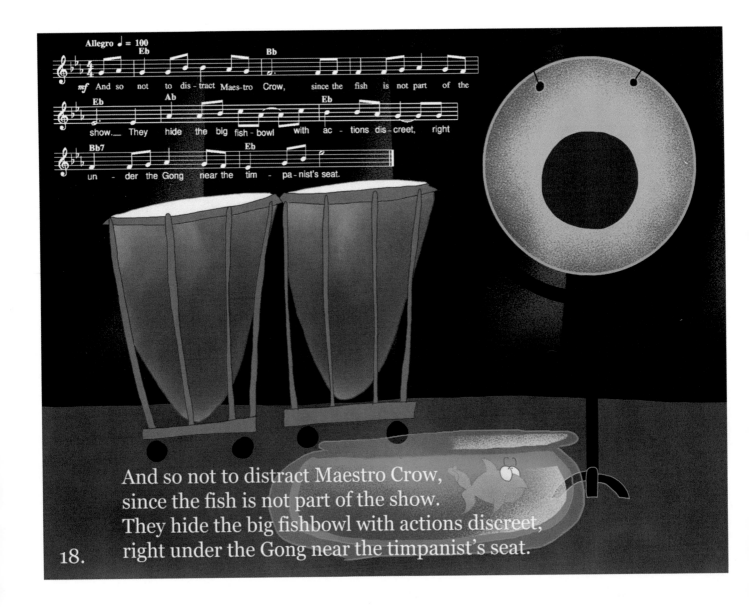

And so not to distract Maestro Crow,
since the fish is not part of the show.
They hide the big fishbowl with actions discreet,
right under the Gong near the timpanist's seat.

18.

The animals sit straight and wait to go on, and watch the Conductor take up his baton.

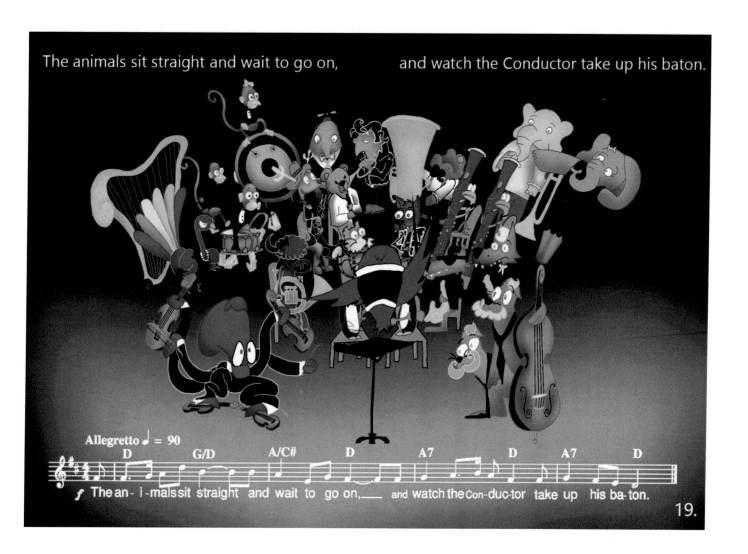

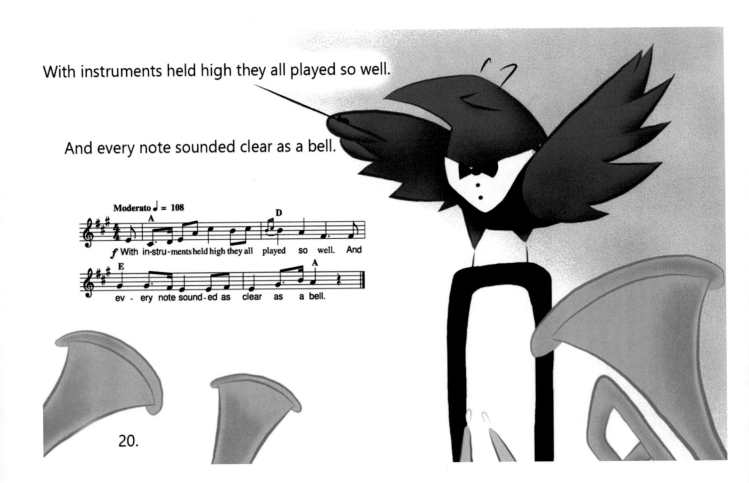

With instruments held high they all played so well.

And every note sounded clear as a bell.

Moderato ♩ = 108

f With in-stru-ments held high they all played so well. And ev - ery note sound-ed as clear as a bell.

20.

As the concert approaches the big Grand Finale,
the Principal monkey can no longer dally.

On top of the gong rack awaiting his cue,
he picks up the mallet and knows what to do.

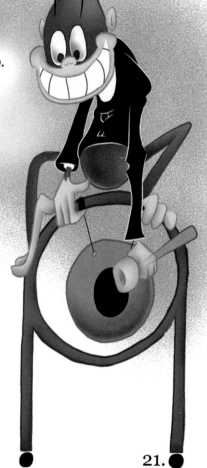

The music soon nears its loud rowdy conclusion,
but what happens next is no magic illusion.
And striking the Gong
with a force OH so strong,
creates a great BONG sound,
but something
goes wrong!

The Gong it fell down, but not to the ground.

It splashed in the fishbowl which muffled the sound. The goldfish was shocked and swam 'round and around.

With eyes opened wide as it jumped up and down.

23.

"Something is wrong," it cried out with a fright! "There's a Gong in my fishbowl, that's simply not right!"

Allegro ♩ = 120

Dm ... Gm ...

𝆑 "Some - thing is wrong," it cried out with a fright! "There's a

Gm ... Dm ... Dm ... E ... A

Gong in my fish - bowl, ___ that's simp - ly not right!"

𝆑𝆑

24.

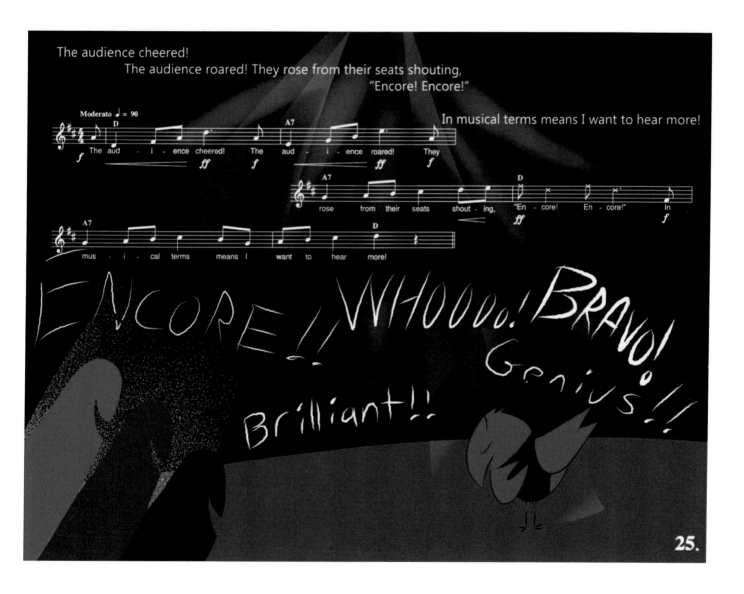

25.

26.

To the monkey's surprise, the whole crowd did agree, they never, not ever, not one time you see, heard a symphony ending so clever and funky. Thanks to the slap happy orchestra monkey.

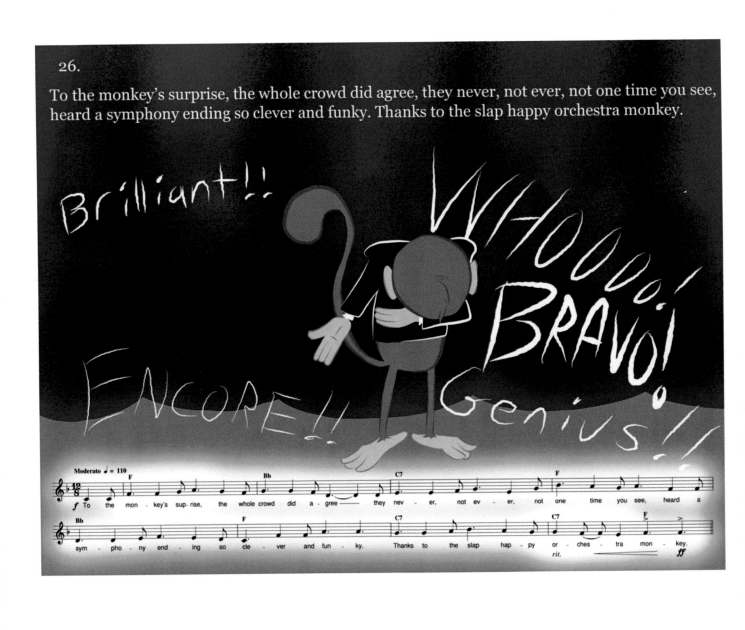

Anthony J. Cirone - San Francisco Symphony, Author

Marie Colligan – Romance Novel Author

Elizabeth A. Bongiorno - Music Composer, Pianist

Daniel Evans - Illustrator

Anthony M. Bongiorno – Vocals, Timpani, Percussion

Printed in the United States
by Baker & Taylor Publisher Services